Who's Afraid of MONSTERS?

By Mary Tillworth
Illustrated by Joe Mathieu

A Random House PICTUREBACK® Book

Random House 🏠 New York

"Sesame Workshop,"® "Sesame Street,"® and associated characters, trademarks, and design elements
are owned and licensed by Sesame Workshop. © 2016 by Sesame Workshop. All Rights Reserved.
Published in the United States by Random House Children's Books, a division of Penguin Random House LLC, 1745 Broadway,
New York, NY 10019, and in Canada by Penguin Random House Canada Limited, Toronto, in conjunction with Sesame Workshop.
Pictureback, Random House, and the Random House colophon are registered trademarks of Penguin Random House LLC.
randomhousekids.com
SesameStreetBooks.com
www.sesamestreet.org
Educators and librarians, for a variety of teaching tools, visit us at RHTeachersLibrarians.com
ISBN 978-1-101-93840-9 (trade) — ISBN 978-1-101-93841-6 (ebook)
MANUFACTURED IN CHINA
10 9 8 7 6 5 4 3 2 1
Random House Children's Books supports the First Amendment and celebrates the right to read.

On Halloween morning, Elmo was poking around in his closet.

"What should Elmo be for Halloween?" Elmo wondered.

Suddenly, the bedroom door creaked open. Elmo turned and jumped!

"Fooled you! It's me!" Abby said with a giggle. "I'm ready for trick-or-treating!"

Elmo was glad that it wasn't a *real* monster!

"Abby scared Elmo," Elmo said. "But just a little bit. Elmo wants to be a very scary monster for Halloween!"

"Any luck in finding a costume, Elmo?" Elmo's mommy asked.

"Does Abby think a scarecrow is scary?" Elmo
asked. Abby shook her head no.

"What about a giant kitty cat?" Elmo continued.
"Or maybe a superhero?"
Elmo's mommy looked thoughtful.

"I know," said Abby. "I'll practice my magic on you!"

"Okay," Elmo replied.

"Monster, donster, diddle, diddle, ponster," Abby rhymed. "Make Elmo into a scary . . . MONSTER!"

And there was Elmo, in a pumpkin suit just like Abby's.

"Oh, Abby," Elmo said, giggling. "Now Elmo is a funny-looking pumpkin! Not even a scary jack-o'-lantern!"

"Sorry, Elmo," Abby apologized. "I'll try to change you back."

"That's okay, Abby," Elmo said. "I know you were trying to be kind and helpful."

"Maybe we can find a scary costume at the party store," Elmo's mommy suggested as she helped Elmo out of the pumpkin suit.

Abby, Elmo, and Elmo's mommy left for the store. They hadn't gone far when Elmo spotted a giant blue monster walking stiffly toward them.

"A monster!" Elmo cried.

Me want cookies!

Elmo, Abby, and Elmo's mommy started to laugh.
They had figured out who the monster was!

Cooookies!

It's only Cookie Monster!

Phew!

As they headed farther down Sesame Street, they heard a strange buzzing sound.

"What's that funny sound?" Elmo whispered.

"I don't know," Abby whispered back. "But it's a little bit scary!"

BUZZ-ZZ-ZZ-ZZ!

Out jumped Grover.

"It is I, Grover," he said, "disguised as a bumblebee—a super-scary bumblebee! Bzzzzz!"

"Oh, Grover!" Elmo said. "You make Elmo laugh. You're not scary at all!"

At the party store, Elmo, Elmo's mommy, and Abby saw
Big Bird. He was also looking for a Halloween costume.

Suddenly, they came face to face with a friendly-looking witch. This time, no one was scared. They saw right away that the witch was Zoe.

R.I.P.

"Can you think of a good scary costume?" Elmo asked Zoe.
"Hmm," Zoe said, twirling as she thought. "What about a—"
"Mummy!" cried Elmo.
"One mummy, ah, ah, ah!" the Count said with a chuckle.

Zoe put her arm around Elmo. "Oh, Elmo," she said kindly. "You're shaking like that crazy skeleton!" She pointed to a skeleton that was rattling as if it was doing a funny dance.

"That's it!" Elmo cried. "Elmo will be a skeleton for Halloween! That way, Elmo can shake and rattle—and be really scary!"

Finally, it was time for everyone to go trick-or-treating. What a spooky group they were: a big blue monster, a mummy, a bumblebee, a witch, a jack-o'-lantern, and one very rattly skeleton!

Just then, a HUGE dinosaur stomped into view.
"It's a *real* monster this time!" Abby cried. "And
it's really BIG!"

Elmo took a deep breath. "Nothing can scare *Elmo*!"
Elmo said, and bravely walked up to the enormous dinosaur.

"Aaahhh! A skeleton!" cried the dinosaur. "It's too SCARY!"

"Hi, Snuffy," Elmo said. "It's Elmo! Elmo's not really a skeleton!"

Oh!

Phew!

Snuffy!

TRICK OR TREAT!

Then . . . all of a sudden . . .

. . . a big ghost came blowing down Sesame Street.

This ghost was really something! And then everyone
noticed its feet—and they realized who the ghost was.
They all laughed.

NOBODY was afraid of monsters anymore!

✹ MAKE THE MASKS
◉ HANG UP THE POSTER

✹ Ask a grown-up to remove the masks from the book and help you attach short strings to both sides where indicated. The masks should be tied around your forehead, above your ears.

◉ Remove the poster along the perforated line, and unfold it carefully. Tape it to a wall or door for a great Halloween decoration.

HAPPY HALLOWEEN

And . . . BOO!